CURVEBALL

DISCARDED

WINNING SEASON

CURVEBALL

RICH WALLACE

SCHOLASTIC INC.

New York Toronto London Auckland Sydney
Mexico City New Delhi Hong Kong Buenos Aires

ISBN-13: 978-0-545-08607-3
ISBN-10: 0-545-08607-8

12 11 10 9 8 7 6 5 4 3 2 1   8 9 10 11 12 13/0

Printed in the U.S.A.   40

First Scholastic printing, May 2008

Set in Caslon 224 Book

FOR JACOB

CURVEBALL

· CONTENTS ·

1

Two Runs Down

Eddie Ventura scanned the infield, then dug his toe into the dirt near first base. His right hand was sweating inside his glove despite the cool afternoon breeze.

Everyone in the dugout and the bleachers was standing, waiting for Ramiro Velez to deliver the crucial pitch.

Eddie took a deep breath and went into a crouch, ready to dart toward any ball that was hit or thrown his way. The Hudson City Hornets had to get this next hitter out.

"Let's go, Ramiro!" Eddie called. "No batter!"

Ramiro turned his head slightly toward Eddie, and a faint smile crossed his lips. Eddie hardly ever said anything.

Hoboken had runners at second and third with two outs in the top of the final inning. Hudson City would get one more at-bat, but the Hornets were already two runs behind.

Ramiro leaned back, kicked up his leg, and hurled the ball toward the plate. The batter swung hard, but the ball smacked into catcher Jared Owen's mitt for strike three.

Ramiro shook his fist.

"Yes!" said Eddie as they raced off the field.

"Big rally now," Spencer Lewis said to Eddie as they grabbed their bats from the rack. "We need some base runners."

Spencer was the team's best hitter and biggest talker, but the Hornets needed to get at least two men on base or Spencer wouldn't even bat.

And things didn't look good as Willie Shaw

popped the first pitch lazily toward second base. Eddie groaned with the rest of the Hornets as the fielder easily caught the ball.

Lamont Wilkins struck out, and just like that the Hornets were down to their last out.

Jared stepped up to the plate. Eddie shut his eyes quickly, then moved to the on-deck circle.

Relax, Eddie told himself. *Time to do something big here.*

Eddie was a fair hitter—a lefty—but no way was he one of the stars. He'd had three singles in the first six games and had drawn a couple of walks. But he'd never been one to really come through in the clutch the way Spencer or Jared always seemed to.

The Hornets had lost their first four games this season, but they were presently riding a modest two-game winning streak. A third straight victory today would be an enormous boost, but a loss would put them back in a deep hole.

Eddie's tall, thin build didn't provide much

power, except in his imagination. *On deck for the Hudson City Hornets—EDDIEEE Ven-TUR-a,* he thought, sounding to himself like one of the broadcasters for the New York Yankees. *If Jared can get on base here, the hard-hitting Ventura will surely make something happen.*

A burst of cheers broke Eddie from his thoughts, and he looked up to see Jared sprinting toward first base. Eddie gripped the bat tighter.

Jared rounded first and kept on going, sliding safely into second with a double.

Spencer stepped out of the dugout and gave Eddie a firm punch on the shoulder. "Grind time, Mr. Ventura," Spencer said. "It's up to you now, boss."

Eddie swallowed hard. He walked to the plate and took a practice swing. He heard that imaginary radio voice again: *Ventura could homer and tie this game with one swing of the bat.* But then again, he'd never hit a home run in his life.

The pitcher took the throw from the second

baseman and turned to face Eddie. He squinted and glared. Eddie glared back, trying to look tougher than he felt.

This guy had struck Eddie out twice today. He had a wicked fastball and a decent curve. But he had to be tiring by now.

Jared took a short lead off second base. Eddie drew back his bat and waited. The first pitch was low and outside. Ball one.

"Good eye, Eddie!" came a cry.

The second pitch was high and outside. Eddie stepped out of the batter's box and glanced toward the Hornets' dugout.

"A walk's as good as a hit," Coach Wimmer called.

Eddie let out his breath. It was true. He didn't need a home run. He didn't even need a single. All he had to do was get on base and keep this inning alive.

Eddie crouched a little lower and inched closer to the plate, trying to shrink his strike zone. The third pitch looked good, maybe a little low, but right down the center of the plate.

Eddie didn't flinch. The umpire called, "Ball three!" and the pitcher shook his head in frustration.

The Hoboken catcher turned to the umpire.

"It was low," the umpire said.

The catcher called time and jogged to the mound to talk to the pitcher. Eddie's teammates were rattling the fence in front of their dugout. Spencer was grinning confidently at Eddie from the on-deck circle. "Gut check!" Spencer said. "Be the man."

Eddie wiped his sweaty palms on his uniform pants. A hundred things crossed his mind at once. Nobody swung on a 3–0 count, so the pitcher would be playing it safe. He'd groove one right down the middle. Eddie could bunt it, then run like mad toward first base.

Or, he thought, *This kid Ventura has the ability to hit away, driving the ball deep into the outfield and bringing Jared home.*

Or he could play it safe, too, like he knew he was supposed to. Take the pitch even if it was a strike.

And here it came, waist-high but inside. Eddie leaned back as the ball whizzed by.

"Ball four," called the umpire. "Take your base."

Eddie couldn't help but smile as he jogged toward first. The dugout fence was shaking and rattling again; Miguel and Lamont and the others were yelling his name.

The Hoboken coach walked to the mound and chatted with the pitcher, but he left him in the game.

Eddie stepped off first base, tensed and ready to sprint all the way home if he needed to.

Here came the pitch, here came the *smack* as Spencer connected, the *Oooh* from the spectators, and the roar from the Hudson City dugout as the ball shot deep into right field. Eddie ran hard, but he turned slightly to watch as the ball sailed over the fence and into the parking lot.

That's gone! said the announcer in his mind.

Eddie threw his arms straight over his head and laughed as he stepped on second base. He watched Jared leap onto home plate, then rounded third and raced home to do the same. And with all of his teammates, he waited for Spencer and his enormous, triumphant grin.

They mobbed him. Three straight wins. The Hornets were definitely back in business.

2

Deep in Thought

Eddie was taking his books out of his locker the next morning when Calvin Tait walked up and grabbed his arm.

"What's up, Tait?" Eddie asked.

"I need a favor, Ventura. I need an article on yesterday's baseball game by this afternoon, and I don't have time to write it. I still have to write up Monday's softball game, and I've got a track meet of my own right after school."

"So?"

"So Mr. Lobianco says you're an awesome writer.

Plus you're on the team. Can you give me three hundred words by one o'clock?"

"I never wrote a sports article before," Eddie mumbled.

"No time like now to start. You guys won yesterday, right? It'll be easy."

Calvin was the newly appointed sports editor of the school paper, *The Hornet Highlights*. In fact, he was the entire staff of the sports department. Every week he wrote short articles about each team's results. The paper was usually just four pages, with one page devoted to sports. It was printed right from a computer at the school and was distributed on Wednesday mornings.

Eddie thought it over for a moment. He loved reading *Sports Illustrated* and the coverage of the Yankees and Knicks and Giants in the *New York Post*. This might be fun. And he could probably get some free time to write at the end of English class, especially since Mr. Lobianco was the adviser to the newspaper. He could finish the article at lunch.

"All right, I'll do it," Eddie said.

"You're the man," Calvin said. "I'll make sure you get a byline."

"No. I don't want one," Eddie said.

A byline would identify him as the writer of the article: "By Eddie Ventura." Spencer and the others would get on him about that for sure.

"I'd rather nobody knew who wrote it," Eddie said. "Keep it a secret. Or even better, just let them think you wrote it. You write everything else in that section."

"Whatever you want," Calvin said. "I'll owe you one."

Eddie made some notes about the game during math class, jotting down the name of the winning pitcher, the team's record, a few things Coach Wimmer had said after the game. When he reached the classroom for English, Mr. Lobianco was waiting for him at the doorway.

"Calvin told me you're going to help us out," the teacher said. "Tell you what: how about if I write you a pass to the computer lab and you can work on the article now?"

"Sounds great."

So Eddie walked to the computer lab and took a seat at one of the terminals.

He'd read hundreds of sports articles in the past few years, but that didn't seem to make it any easier to get started on one.

What was the most important thing about that game? he wondered. *That should be my lead.*

Eddie started typing:

The Hudson City seventh-grade base-ball team took a big step forward Tuesday, rallying in the bottom of the final inning to beat Hoboken, 6–5.

The victory moved the Hornets' record to three wins and four losses and placed them back in contention for the league title. It was the team's third straight win after a rocky beginning to the season.

Okay, Eddie thought. *So much for the basics.* Now he needed to insert some play-by-play excitement into the article. Mr. Lobianco always said, "Write what you know best." So Eddie thought hard about what he'd been feeling in that final inning.

The Hornets trailed by two runs in the seventh when first baseman Eddie Ventura sparked a late rally that led to the win. After Jared Owen reached second base with a double, Ventura stepped to the plate.

With every eye in the ballpark focused on the batter, Ventura dug in and glared at Hoboken's best pitcher. It was clear that Ventura's cool, calm stare rattled the hurler, who threw four shaky pitches that were all out of the strike zone. Ventura had drawn a walk! He flipped his bat toward the dugout and confidently jogged to first base.

```
    The  next  batter,  Spencer  Lewis,
finished  the  job  with  a  game-winning
three-run  homer.
```

Eddie stopped typing and looked around the lab. A copy of that day's *New York Times* newspaper was sitting on a table. He grabbed it and turned to the sports section.

He read through an article on yesterday's Yankees-Tigers game, then glanced at an interview with the Knicks' coach.

Quotes, Eddie told himself. *All of these articles include comments from the key players.*

He could interview Spencer or Ramiro, perhaps, but he was running out of time. So he decided to quote himself. He started typing again.

```
    "I  knew  I  had  to  get  on  base,"
Ventura  said  after  the  game.  "If  he'd
thrown  a  good  pitch,  I  would  have
nailed  it,  but  as  Coach  Wimmer  always
```

tells us, 'A walk is as good as a hit.'
I was just happy to do my part to get
us the victory."

Pitcher Ramiro Velez was credited
with the win for the Hornets in relief
of starter Miguel Rivera.

Next up for the Hornets is Friday's
game at Weehawken.

Eddie looked at the clock. He'd been writing for nearly an hour! He was already late for his next class.

He quickly e-mailed the article to Calvin and gathered his books. Fortunately his next class was history—taught by Coach Wimmer.

Coach was standing in front of the class talking as Eddie quietly slipped into the room.

Coach raised his eyebrows, and his fat, pink face stretched into a grin. "Nice of you to show up, Eddie," he said. "You're only fifteen minutes late."

Eddie blushed. "I was, um, doing something for Mr. Lobianco," he said.

Coach Wimmer rubbed his bald head with his fingertips. "So he wrote you a pass?"

"Yeah. But . . . the pass was for last period. I turned it in at the computer lab. I lost track of time."

Coach nodded and gave Eddie a sarcastic-looking smile. "I guess that bell isn't loud enough, huh?"

"I sort of didn't hear it," Eddie said quietly. "I was deep in thought."

Most of the class laughed at that.

"Eddie's a deep thinker, all right," Spencer said.

"He's like a philosopher or something," said Lamont. "He thinks a lot more than he talks."

"He'd better be thinking more," Spencer said, "because he almost never says anything."

Coach just rolled his eyes and shook his head. "Where were we?" he said. And he got right back to the lecture.

That was one of the things Eddie and the other

players loved about Coach Wimmer—he knew when to cut them a break. He'd been coaching and teaching for so long that he knew how kids' minds worked. They wanted to do the right thing, but it didn't always come out as planned. Coach could always laugh at the mess-ups, especially when he saw that an honest effort had been made.

Eddie let out his breath and opened his notebook. A ball of paper hit him on the arm. He tossed it back at Spencer and grinned.

Eddie didn't mind getting busted by the guys. He knew he was the quietest player on the team. He didn't quite know why he was so quiet, especially considering his family.

Eddie's father was a lawyer, and his mother was a third-grade teacher. They talked all day long for a living. His older brother, Lenny, was a student across the river at New York University and was also thinking about going to law school. And his sister, Irene, was president of the junior class at Hudson City High School. So it didn't figure much that Eddie wasn't a talker, except that it was hard for him to get a word in at all in a household like that.

It didn't matter to him. Let the other people do the talking; he just loved to play baseball.

3

Instincts

Eddie could feel the excitement building as the bus climbed Palisades Avenue toward the Weehawken field. Those four straight losses at the beginning of the season felt like a long time ago; this team definitely had momentum now.

Outside the bus windows, the Hudson River was reflecting the sun. The George Washington Bridge loomed large in the distance. This stretch of New Jersey along the Hudson River was one of the most densely populated areas in the country.

"Finally got some of that sunshine breaking

through," Spencer said to Eddie as the bus rolled into the parking lot. "About time, I'd say. Seems like every game we've played it's been cold or drizzly. Or both."

Eddie nodded.

"I need to get that warmth in the muscles," Spencer said. "You know what I'm saying? More power."

"Yeah," Eddie said.

Spencer stretched out his arms in front of him. "Be hitting that ball all over the place today, I think. Feeling good. You?"

"Sure," Eddie said. "I feel good."

"Time to even up that record." Spencer stood and stepped into the aisle. "Hammer that little ball over the fence a few times."

Eddie gave a tight smile and nodded again.

"Just don't tire yourself out with all that jabbering you're doing," Spencer said, rolling his eyes.

Miguel leaned over from the seat in front of Eddie. "Yeah, Ventura," he said. "Don't you ever shut up? I counted six words out of you on the ride over here. That must be some kind of record."

"No," Spencer said. "His record for most words at one time is that quote he gave Calvin for the school paper the other day. That was, like, three whole sentences. Anyway, Eddie, I'm the one who hit the home run. What's he quoting you for?"

Eddie laughed. "I don't know. Calvin had this deadline. . . . I just happened to be around when he needed me."

Eddie had a poor day with his bat, grounding out three times and striking out once. But it didn't matter, as the Hornets built a big lead early and pitcher David Choi was nearly unhittable.

So all that was left as the Hornets took the field for the bottom of the seventh inning was to preserve the shutout.

David was sweating heavily, but his pitches still had plenty of speed. He looked focused and confident as he struck out the first two batters. There was lots of chatter from the Hornets' infielders.

"Mow 'em down!" yelled Miguel from his short-stop position.

"No batter," called Lamont from second base.

Eddie swallowed hard and swept his foot through the dirt in front of him. It had been a very routine day in the field for him. A handful of put-outs on throws from the other infielders, one easy pop-up that he caught in foul territory. And Weehawken had only had three base runners, so there hadn't been much activity on that end, either.

But he stayed alert. One more out and this one would be over.

Ventura really sets the tone for this infield, the announcer's voice in his head was saying. *Always calm but always ready. The kid's got Major League instincts.*

David went into his windup and delivered the pitch. The Weehawken batter swung hard but only managed to top the ball, and it bounced quickly toward the gap to Eddie's right.

Eddie lunged toward the ball and got his glove on it, stopping it as he fell to one knee. He scooped up the ball and raced toward first base as the batter ran up the base path. David was running toward the base, too, but Eddie decided not to throw the ball. He was closer to the base than the batter.

He reached first base a half step before the batter, landing with his left foot and hopping back to avoid a collision.

The umpire called the batter out, and Eddie tossed the ball to David with a grin. "Great pitching!" he said.

Superb effort from Ventura, said that radio voice. *A game-clinching play, for sure.*

"Nice hustle, Eddie," David said as he was lifted off his feet by Jared. All of the Hornets were on the field now, celebrating win number four.

Eddie let out his breath. His heart was beating fast. He followed his happy teammates to the bus.

"All right, good effort," Coach Wimmer said, standing in the aisle and gripping the overhead railing with one hand as the bus lurched forward. "A couple more like that and we'll be contenders."

"Coach of the year!" called Miguel.

Coach blushed. "Yes, Miguel, I'm certain that the Hall of Fame will be inducting me any day now," he joked. "Okay, enjoy this win. We'll get back to work tomorrow. You guys aren't ready for the World Series yet, believe me."

Sunday night Eddie sat at the computer terminal in the family room, pondering his next article for Wednesday's school paper. He'd promised Calvin that he'd turn it in on Monday morning.

"School project?" asked his mother, looking into the room.

"Not really. Something for the newspaper."

"Wonderful," she said. Mom was big on extra-curricular stuff. All of the Ventura kids had been encouraged to play musical instruments and get involved in school clubs and other activities.

With Eddie, it had been mostly sports. He'd taken some piano lessons in second grade, but all the repetition bored him silly. He got out of that by promising to join the Cub Scouts. And soon he'd gotten out of Cub Scouts by promising to join the junior choir at church.

That hadn't lasted long, either. This time it wasn't his choice; his singing was so flat and quiet that the choir director asked him to leave.

But he always stuck with sports. From his first season of Little League baseball, he'd known this was for him. Now maybe he'd found something else, too. Writing for the paper seemed like fun.

"Don't forget to take the trash cans out tonight," Mom said.

"No problem. As soon as I'm done writing."

He had done some studying that afternoon of the articles in the sports sections of the *Hudson Dispatch* and the *New York Times*. The most interesting articles did a lot more than just give the score and the major details of the games. They seemed to put Eddie right there in the moment, making him feel like a part of the action.

He decided to try that, too. It shouldn't be too

hard, he figured, since he really *had* been part of the action.

Bam.

The baseball rocketed off the Weehawken hitter's bat like a speeding bullet, zinging toward right field.

That's a double for sure! the fans must have been thinking.

But quick as lightning, Hudson City first baseman Eddie Ventura dove for the ball as it skipped toward the outfield. With his arm stretched like a rubber band, Ventura managed to knock the ball down with his glove. Then, scrambling to his feet, he scooped up the ball and raced toward first base, getting there a mere step ahead of the speedy Weehawken hitter.

"Out!" yelled the umpire.

Game over! Hudson City 7, Weehawken 0. Another big win for the Hornets!

Pitcher David Choi went the distance to earn the victory, allowing just two hits. Spencer Lewis and Miguel Rivera each had run-scoring doubles for the Hornets.

"It's a whole new season now," Coach Wimmer told his players after the game.

With their record even at four wins and four losses, the Hornets are steadily moving up in the standings. "We're as good as any team in the league," said Coach, who thinks he may be headed for the Hall of Fame soon. "Now we just have to prove it."

The Hornets will have a chance to do just that when they host league-leading Liberty Junior High School of Jersey City this afternoon.

Not bad, Eddie thought as he read his work over. *This kid might turn out to be a great sportswriter, too. That's some combination of brains and athletic talent at work right there. He's certainly worth keeping an eye on.*

4

Big Doings

Eddie walked toward home plate Wednesday afternoon before the game, ready to take some batting practice. He noticed David Choi sitting in the dugout, intently reading the school paper.

David was reading the back page—the sports section. Eddie stopped for a moment to see David's reaction.

"Wow," David said with an amused look as he set down the paper. "How much did you pay Calvin to write that one, Ventura?"

Eddie gave a sly smile and shrugged. "Calvin's in

my math class." That was true, of course, but it had nothing to do with the situation.

"I throw a two-hit shutout and he writes about you fielding a ground ball!" David said. He shook his head but laughed. "I'll have to have a little talk with that guy."

"Ah, leave him alone," Eddie said. "Calvin has to write the entire sports section."

"Okay, well let's give him something good to write about again." David picked up his glove and started walking toward the outfield. It was Miguel's turn to pitch today.

Liberty was 7–1 and well ahead of the pack in the league standings. They were a near certainty to make the playoffs. Things weren't anywhere near as sure for Hudson City, but they were definitely on an upswing.

So when the Hornets took the field for the first inning, it was with a great deal of enthusiasm and confidence. But they were also feeling pressure.

Big game for the Hornets, Eddie thought as he

jogged toward first base. *Over at first, you've got Eddie Ventura, who's been rock-solid in the field all season. This kid's got poise and skills that can take him a long way. Maybe all the way to the Majors.*

But this is a big test this afternoon. Liberty's been the class of the league so far. The Hornets have got to be at the top of their game to have any chance at all.

And it turned out that both teams were at their best, at least defensively. Miguel held Liberty scoreless through the first four innings. But his Liberty counterpart was doing even better—Hudson City had only had one base runner.

Eddie had struck out on three pitches his first time up, but he had a good feeling as he stepped into the on-deck circle. He'd been studying this pitcher's pattern.

The guy was on the short side, but he had long arms that allowed for a sweeping overhand pitching style that was difficult to judge. He had started every batter with a wide, diving curveball that looked as if it would be way outside but broke sharply at the last second. Then, with the batter bracing for another confusing curve, he blazed a fastball right by him.

It had worked well so far. Nearly every Hudson City batter had either swung wildly at that first pitch or stood still as it veered over the plate for a strike.

And as Eddie watched, the Liberty pitcher threw that curve to Jared. Maybe Jared was expecting it, too, because he held his ground. And this time the pitch curved too far inside, nipping Jared just below his shoulder.

Jared dropped his bat and winced, rubbing that spot. But he turned and winked at Eddie, then trotted to first base.

Finally, an opportunity for the Hornets to break through with a run, Eddie thought. *This kid Ventura is smart and patient. You can expect some big doings here, fans.*

The Hudson City dugout had come alive with shouts of "Let's go, Eddie!" and "Move him over!"

Eddie knew that his task was to get Jared to second base. He dug in and waited for the pitch, eager to see if the pitcher would stick with that same pattern.

Here came that big curve, as expected. Eddie took the pitch for a strike, then made a show of looking frustrated and confused. He wanted to make sure the pitcher thought he'd fooled him again and would follow up with the fastball.

Coach Wimmer was flashing Eddie the bunt sign. Jared would be running on the pitch.

As the pitcher's arm came forward, Jared took off for second. Eddie squared himself in the box and held out the bat, gently tapping the ball toward third base.

A terrific bunt, perfectly placed.

Eddie ran at top speed up the base path. The ball arrived just before he did. He was out, but the sacrifice had worked. Jared was safe at second with only one out, and Spencer was coming up to bat.

"Beautiful job!" Coach Wimmer said as Eddie entered the dugout. Lamont smacked him on the back, and Willie gave him a high five.

Outstanding play by Ventura, as we've come to expect, Eddie thought. *That could be the key moment of the game right there.*

Spencer continued his clutch hitting, smacking a line-drive single up the middle to bring Jared home. That proved to be all the Hornets needed, as they shut Liberty down for three more innings to earn a tight 1–0 victory.

Eddie was beaming as the players shook hands after the game. He really had played a huge role in setting up that game-winning run. He was already thinking about his next article for the paper. They'd beaten the best team in the league!

There was no better feeling than helping his team win. He had spoken louder with his actions than he ever did with his voice.

* * *

"So let's hit some grub spot," Spencer was saying to Miguel and Jared in the locker room after the game. "Celebrate this big win with some fajitas, maybe."

Spencer looked over at Eddie, who was sitting on the bench in front of his locker, one shoe on and one shoe off. "You hungry, Ventura?" Spencer asked. "Up for some Mexican or something?"

"Sure." Eddie took out his wallet and looked inside. It was empty. "I got, like, thirty cents," he said. "You spot me some cash?"

"At ten percent interest," Spencer replied. "Anybody else want to come? The train's pulling out."

No one else could make it, so Eddie walked with the three others on the wide Boulevard sidewalk toward El Torito. They were all still wearing their red-and-white uniforms and baseball hats.

"Hold on, guys," Eddie said as they reached Twelfth Street. "I can maybe get some money from my dad."

The law office—Ventura and Zambrano, Attorneys/Abogados—was on the second floor of a building in the middle of the block, above a computer store. Eddie opened the door and led the boys up the steep, narrow stairs.

Mr. Ventura was in his office, typing at a computer terminal. He had short curly hair, mostly silver in color, and a stockier build than his son. He stood up and stepped out from around his desk, which was piled high with papers. "Well, this an honor," he said with a smile. "We've got the heart of the lineup visiting, huh?"

"That's us," Spencer said.

"So how'd it go?" Mr. Ventura asked. "Did you beat those guys?"

"Big-time," Spencer replied. "Miguel was the man. Shut down the best team in the league, right?"

Mr. Ventura turned to his son. "How did you do, Eddie?"

"Flawless," Spencer said before Eddie could

speak. "Laid down a nice bunt to set up the winning run. The *only* run."

"Probably be the headline in next week's paper," Miguel said. "'Ventura Bunts Hornets to Victory.' And, oh, by the way," he continued, "some kid named Rivera pitched a three-hit shutout. Maybe they'll squeeze that in at the end, after a few paragraphs about Eddie's heroics."

Eddie blushed but grinned. Miguel had a point. His article might have to focus on someone else's contributions this week.

Mr. Ventura laughed. He knew that his son wanted to remain an anonymous reporter, but he could see that the secret might not last much longer.

"Well," Eddie said, "like I was saying, Calvin had those deadlines. . . ."

"And you just happened to be in the right place," Spencer said.

"That's about it. Anyway, Dad, could you give me a few bucks? We were going to get a little snack on the way home."

"Why not? A game-winning bunt has to be worth something."

"Worth at least twenty bucks," Spencer said.

"How about five?" Mr. Ventura said. "A home run, now that'd be worth twenty."

"Thanks," Eddie said as his father handed him a bill. "You working late again?"

"Nope. Leaving in five minutes. You're lucky you caught me."

On the wall behind Mr. Ventura was a large photograph of the whole family from several years before. Eddie, about age six, was smiling broadly, and his top two front teeth were missing. He was wearing a blue suit jacket and a blue-and-yellow-striped tie, and his dark hair was buzzed nearly to the scalp.

Miguel pointed at the picture. "Now your brother and sister, *they're* good athletes," he kidded Eddie. "Guess they got all the talent, huh?"

"Guess so," Eddie said. "There was only so much to go around."

"Too bad," Spencer said. "You were one handsome dude back then, too. What happened?"

"Got old and ugly," Eddie said. "Like my old man."

Mr. Ventura laughed again and pointed toward the door. "Get of here and let me finish writing this memo so I can get home to dinner. I'm starving."

"Us, too," said Jared. "We're gone."

The four boys slipped into a booth near the front of El Torito, and a waitress immediately brought over some chips and salsa.

"I'd love to have some guacamole with that, please," Spencer said.

"Sure thing," she said.

"*Very* nice manners, Spence," Jared kidded.

"I try." Spencer popped his fist down lightly in front of Miguel. "Your uncle here tonight?" he asked.

Miguel's aunt and uncle owned the restaurant. Spencer's implication was clear: if Uncle Victor knew they were there, he might send out some freebies.

"He's always here," Miguel replied. "And believe me, he always knows who else is in here, too. But this is a business. He can't be giving away the house."

Jared nudged Eddie. "We should have worn our El Torito shirts."

Eddie and Jared had played on a YMCA basketball team the summer before that was sponsored by the restaurant.

Spencer put up his hands as if to surrender. "No problemo, boss. But your uncle's been very generous in the past."

"And the present, and the future," Miguel said. "Don't worry. Here he comes."

They turned to see Victor coming their way with a pitcher of soda. Victor was a large guy. He went back and forth from the kitchen to the booths and tables to the cash register near the front. He was always dressed neat in a starched white shirt. He let out a whoop when his eyes locked with his nephew's.

"There's the king of the mound!" he said. "I heard, I heard. Complete game shutout. Not too shabby."

He set the soda on the table. "On the house," he said. "Refills, too, if you're thirsty enough."

"Thank you."

"*Gracias*, Uncle Victor."

Miguel winked at Spencer. "See?" he said as Uncle Victor made his way back to the kitchen. "He's always generous. But spend some money, too."

"That's why I'm here," Spencer said. "Chips and soda aren't nearly enough to fill my belly. Where's the menu? I'm ready for some serious eating. Something cheesy and spicy. And *big*."

Mr. Ventura was just pulling into the driveway as Eddie approached the house. He stepped out of the car and waited for his son.

"Worked longer than five more minutes, huh?" Eddie said.

"Yeah. That legal brief took longer to write

than I expected. I was glad you guys stopped by, though."

Eddie nodded.

The Venturas' house was on Fifth Street between the Boulevard—which was Hudson City's main business street—and Central Avenue, around the corner from Jefferson Elementary School and a couple of blocks from the high school. Eddie loved being so close to the stores and restaurants, but tucked away on one of the less busy side streets.

"You've got some really cool friends," Mr. Ventura said. "They sure tease you a lot, huh?"

"Yeah, but we all do that."

"That's okay," Mr. Ventura said, stopping on the small front porch. "It's how guys interact. If they *didn't* tease you, then you should be worried."

"Right. That's how it works. I give it right back."

"Do you?"

Eddie thought about that for a second. "Sometimes."

"That's good." Mr. Ventura put his hand on

Eddie's shoulder and gave it a light squeeze. "Sometimes we go a whole week without hearing your voice, it seems."

"I guess," Eddie said with a shrug. "Everybody just seems to talk faster than I do. I mean, the words don't come out so quick with me. It's like I gotta think before I say anything, you know?"

"That's not such a bad thing."

"I know. But guys like you and Lenny and Spencer, everything you say just seems to come out right. And quick, too."

"You'd be surprised. It's not always that way. I get on a tough case and I have to think *real* carefully before I speak. Nothing wrong with that."

"Sure. But it's like that with me all the time. . . . That's one of the things I like about writing. If it doesn't come out right, you just delete it and start over."

Mr. Ventura laughed. "Yep, there's no delete button in real-life conversation. A lot of times we wish there was."

He reached for his keys and unlocked the front door. "You got any appetite left?"

"Yeah. I just had a small chicken taco and some chips."

"Let's see what we've got to eat in here. I'm about to pass out from hunger."

"Sounds good," Eddie said. "I burned off a lot of energy today. I can still eat plenty, believe me."

"The Yankee game starts in twenty minutes. Do you have much homework, or can you watch it with me?"

"I've got some easy math homework, so I can do both."

"Me, too. I didn't quite finish that memo yet. Still have some thinking to do about it."

"Think, eat, and watch the Yankees," Eddie said. "Sounds like a good evening to me."

5

"Major Talent"

When Eddie sat down to write late on Sunday evening, he realized that he had a bit of a dilemma. The Hornets had played two games since his last report—the win over Liberty had been followed by a disappointing loss to Bayonne on Friday. Did Calvin want an article on each game or one piece that included them both?

He clicked HudCityCal on his buddy list and fired off an instant message:

EddieV: u there?
HudCityCal: yeah. hey.

EddieV: played 2 games. u got room 4 2 articles?

HudCityCal: no. just one.

EddieV: ok. I'll combine em.

HudCityCal: I could run the standings if u send them
   2 me.

EddieV: I got em.

HudCityCal: u email me it tonite?

EddieV: sure.

HudCityCal: ok. c u later.

So how should he start this one? The loss stunk, but it was the most recent news. On the other hand, the win streak had to end sometime. Coach said they were still right in the thick of the playoff race.

First thing to do was e-mail Calvin the league standings:

East Hudson League

	W	L
Liberty	8	2
Union City	7	3

Memorial	**6**	**4**
Bayonne	**5**	**5**
Hoboken	**5**	**5**
Hudson City	**5**	**5**
Palisades	**2**	**8**
Weehawken	**2**	**8**

Wednesday's games:
Hudson City at Memorial
Liberty at Palisades
Hoboken at Union City
Weehawken at Bayonne

Calvin often used funny names for his bylines. Since he wrote nearly the entire sports section, he didn't want to have every article begin "By Calvin Tait." So he went by Speedy Gonzalez for the track-and-field articles, Pop Fly for softball, and Bent Racket for tennis. Eddie thought hard about a funny byline for himself. Then he started writing.

By Major Talent

A win and a loss last week left the Hornets' seventh-grade baseball squad right smack in the middle of a hotly contested playoff race. With a 5-5 record, Hudson City is in a three-way tie for fourth place in the East Hudson League standings. Four teams will qualify for the postseason tournament.

Wednesday's gigantic 1-0 triumph over league-leading Liberty had briefly boosted the Hornets into the elite level of the league, but Friday's stunning 5-1 loss to Bayonne brought them right back to Earth. Hudson City came out flat and listless against Bayonne and it cost them big-time.

"I think we had a bit of a letdown after a very tense and emotional win over Liberty," said Don Wimmer, Hudson City's veteran coach. "So we had one

great game and one lousy one. We'll
see how well we can bounce back this
week."

The great game was highlighted by
Miguel Rivera's superb shutout pitching
and Spencer Lewis's clutch RBI single.

The lousy game saw pitcher David
Choi take the loss. The Hornets' only
run came when Willie Shaw tripled in
the fifth inning and scored on Lamont
Wilkins's long fly-out.

That summed it up, but Eddie wasn't very
thrilled with the article. It told the story, but it
wasn't much fun.

One of his favorite parts of the sports articles
in the daily papers were the notes and stats that
were often included at the end under headings
like "Knick Knacks," "Yankee Clippers," or "Mets
Musings." He decided to include a few of his own to
liven up the piece.

HORNET HAMMERINGS: Spencer Lewis is the team leader in home runs (4), runs batted in (17), and awful-smelling socks (uncountable). . . . Reliever Ramiro Velez has been the Hornets' most successful pitcher so far (2–0 record) but the worst singer (an unbearable rendition of Sinatra's "My Way" on the bus ride home from Weehawken). . . . The team's other reliever—lefthander Jimmy Fleming—is nearing the team record for butt splinters after spending three straight games entirely on the bench. . . . Four-foot-ten Willie Shaw is still the shortest centerfielder in league history.

Eddie filed the document and shut off the computer. His sister and parents were watching TV. Lenny had been home for the afternoon but had already taken a bus back into New York.

"Ready to join us, Eddie?" his mom asked.

"What's on?"

"A James Bond movie," Irene said. "You already missed half of it."

"No thanks, then. I'm tired anyway. I'm gonna shower and go to bed."

"Don't forget your ears," Mom said.

"What about them?" Eddie asked. How could he forget that he had ears?

"Don't forget to *wash* them. They were looking grungy the last time I checked."

"Oh."

"Must be from that dusty baseball diamond," Mom said.

Eddie looked toward the ceiling. "I'll scrub 'em."

"The dishwasher needs unloading," Dad called.

"I'll do it first thing in the morning. Before school."

Eddie climbed the stairs and entered the bedroom he'd always shared with Lenny. But Lenny was already a junior in college, and he hadn't spent very many nights at home in the past three years. Eddie missed him, but he was glad to have his own space.

Lenny was eight years older, so Eddie had always been the little kid in the house. He'd been in awe of his brother—especially at sports events when Lenny was a key player. In elementary school, Eddie had felt the prestige of having a brother (and later, a sister) who was a high-school sports star. But now, nearly a teenager himself, Eddie was feeling the pressure of needing to assert himself on the field as well.

He knew that he didn't always live up to the play-by-play he heard in his head during the games. He wasn't quite as calm or as skilled or as powerful as that "announcer" made him out to be. But he was going to be. Someday.

Eddie loved to compete, and he didn't mind hard work. And he truly enjoyed playing baseball—the strategy, the tension, the excitement. It was definitely his favorite sport.

The bedroom was full of trophies and plaques and team pictures—most of them were Lenny's, but a small number belonged to Eddie. Lenny had been a strong player on the Hudson City soccer team, and he had also wrestled and run track. There were blown-up photos of Lenny being inducted into the National Honor Society and posing with his girl-friend at the prom.

Eddie's contributions to the walls were mostly team photos, and certificates for taking part. No championships yet. Certainly no MVP awards.

Across the hall, Irene's walls had pictures of her performing at piano recitals and competing for the high-school debate team. There was also a framed article from the *Hudson Dispatch* highlighting her as the newspaper's athlete of week last January for her outstanding performance on the basketball court.

Lots of great things had happened to the kids in this household. So far, Eddie was still the quiet one.

The quiet one with grungy ears. He stuck a fin-ger in one and twirled it around. He looked at the finger. It was dirty.

So he grabbed some clean clothes and headed for the shower.

6

Flem's Return

The talk on the bus ride to Memorial that
Wednesday was about the latest article in the
school paper.

"'My Way'? Where is Calvin getting this stuff
anyway?"

"He told me he has a 'confidential' source on the
team."

"Must be some bigmouth, huh? Somebody who
doesn't know when to shut up."

"That would be Spencer."

"It ain't me. You think I'd make fun of my own
socks?"

"Maybe it's Miguel."

"Maybe it's Coach Wimmer."

"Not me. I'm the one who thinks I belong in the Hall of Fame, remember?"

"'Major Talent'! What kind of a name is that?"

Eddie squirmed a bit in his seat, but he could tell that no one was angry. In fact, everyone seemed pretty amused by the whole thing.

"We can probably rule out Flem, Willie, and Ramiro, since they were the butt of the jokes," Miguel was saying. "And Jared's not clever enough. . . ."

"Am, too!"

"So it *is* you?"

"Nah. But it *could* have been."

"Lamont maybe."

"I still think it's Jared."

David Choi elbowed Eddie. David had easily figured out that Eddie was the source, but he didn't realize that Eddie was actually writing the articles, too. And Eddie knew David would keep the secret. He'd let the other guys figure it out for themselves.

A good idea had struck Eddie, though. In his

next article, he'd be sure to make fun of himself in his "Hornet Hammerings." That would make him less of a suspect, wouldn't it?

The bus squeaked to a stop next to the Memorial field, and the excited Hudson City players quickly forgot about the newspaper.

"Back on track!" Spencer said. "That loss to Bayonne was, like, forever and three days ago, boys. The playoff run starts *today*. Every game from here on out is huge!"

Memorial was also in the running for the playoffs, so the game was hotly contested from the start. First the Hornets scored, then Memorial got two runs of their own. The lead seemed to change every inning.

"What do you think, Miguel?" Coach Wimmer said as the Hornets came off the field after five innings. Hudson City was protecting a 5–4 lead, but Miguel had walked two batters in the fifth. "How's the arm?"

"Arm's good," Miguel said.

"You seem to be losing some of your control."

"Been pitching a lot lately." Miguel looked toward home plate, where Spencer was taking a few practice cuts. "Whoa, I'm on deck!" He leaped up and grabbed a bat, heading out of the dugout.

Coach Wimmer shook his head. "His arm's turning to spaghetti," he said aloud to no one in particular. "He'll walk everybody in the ballpark if I leave him in there."

Coach looked toward the bench, and his eyes settled on Eddie. "Ventura, you bat ninth this inning. Take Flem out behind the dugout and warm him up."

Jimmy Fleming picked up a baseball and said, "Let's go!" A relief pitcher, he'd been the forgotten man in the lineup lately as David and Miguel had thrown a couple of complete games. It looked like he'd be taking over for Miguel this afternoon.

So Eddie and Flem threw the ball back and forth outside the fence.

"Not so hard yet," Eddie said. "Give your arm time to get warm."

"My arm is on fire!" Flem replied. "I haven't pitched in almost two weeks."

"Still," Eddie said. "Get loose. You've got time."

Fleming was a newcomer to Hudson City; he was just getting to know the guys. Like Eddie, he was a left-hander. And, like Eddie, he was usually pretty quiet.

"You ready, Flem?" Coach Wimmer called a few minutes later.

"Definitely."

"Go ahead in."

So Flem and Eddie jogged onto the field together. Bottom of the sixth, Hudson City still ahead by a run.

Miguel had shifted to third base, sending Ryan Grimes out of the lineup.

"Heavy phlegm alert!" Spencer called as he noticed that Flem had taken the mound. "Preserve that W, man! Shut 'em down."

At first base, Eddie took a deep breath and focused on the batter, ready to react to a line drive or a grounder. A one-run lead was thin as can be.

Lots of tension on that field right now, came the play-by-play voice in his head. *This is where the experience of guys like Ventura and Lewis really makes a difference. The standouts always react well to the pressure.*

Flem was fresh. That was obvious from his first two pitches, which blazed by the batter for strikes.

He's got his stuff today. Smooth and fast.

Eddie relaxed a little. Maybe Flem did, too, because his next pitch was a gift to the batter. Straight down the middle, nothing on it, and the Memorial hitter lined it deep into left-center. It bounced hard just before the fence and smacked back onto the field, sending Willie and David scrambling.

The batter had rounded second before Willie finally came up with the ball. His throw to Miguel was on target, but the batter slid under the tag for a triple. He popped up and brushed the dirt from his pants, grinning widely.

This is trouble. Nobody out and a man on third.

Miguel frowned and tossed the ball back to the pitcher. This had been a troubling pattern when Fleming pitched. Brilliant one moment, vulnerable the next. He'd blown a couple of games during that early losing streak.

Second batter. Again, two pitches, two quick strikes. And then the batter hit a bullet, a line drive up the middle that looked like a certain run-scorer.

Somehow Spencer got to the ball, extending his glove and making an incredible diving catch. He fell to the dirt, rolled to his knees, and fired the ball to Miguel.

The Memorial base runner was caught off guard. He'd streaked toward the plate, assuming the ball would land safely. But Spencer had caught it on the fly. Double play!

"Yeah, Spencer!" Eddie yelled, as loud as anything he'd said all season.

Now that's *Major League ability! Unbelievable play. This entire Hudson City infield—from first base all the way to third—has been spectacular lately.*

Lamont trotted over and slapped hands with Spencer. On the mound, Jimmy Fleming raised his fist and pumped it.

The stunning double play seemed to take away all of Memorial's energy. Jimmy struck out the next batter.

And after the Hornets picked up another run in the top of the seventh, Jimmy put Memorial down in order, sealing the 6–4 win.

All of the talk in the locker room after the game was about Spencer's big play.

"As if this kid needs any more fuel for his ego," Coach Wimmer said with a laugh. "If his head gets any bigger we'll need to special order his caps."

Spencer shook his head with an embarrassed smile. "All in a day's work," he said. "Whatever I gotta do, I do it."

Eddie looked over at Spencer. It was true—the kid talked nonstop, especially about himself. But he backed it up, too. You couldn't argue with that. Baseball, football, basketball—Spencer was always right there in the front line, battling with everything he had. You had to admire a guy like that.

He'd certainly earned it today.

7

Time Off

Thursday was a half-day at school and Coach Wimmer held a brief practice session, so the players had most of the afternoon free.

The temperature was in the high seventies and there was no chance of rain, so Eddie and several others headed down to Hamilton Park, which stretched along the Hudson River on the flats below the town.

Ramiro had a soccer ball and Lamont brought along a Frisbee. But most of the guys just took off their shirts and lay on the grass in the sun.

"Good day to forget all about baseball for a minute," Spencer said, lying with his eyes shut and his arms and legs spread wide.

In the backs of their minds, all of the players knew they had a big game the next day against Palisades. But Spencer was right. They needed a break from the pressure.

Eddie took off his socks and sneakers and sat looking across the river at the huge skyscrapers on the Manhattan skyline. Directly across from Hudson City were the many large piers and shipping terminals.

As close as they lived to New York City, Eddie had only been there a handful of times. His parents went in often for dinner or shows, and of course, his brother lived there. His parents had taken him to a couple of Knicks games at Madison Square Garden and baseball games at Yankee Stadium, and they'd been to some of the museums. But Eddie couldn't picture himself living there.

After a while, Calvin Tait came walking up. Eddie was relieved to see that he was with Danielle

Rosado. If Calvin had been alone, the guys would have grilled him about the baseball articles. With a girl around, they'd just try to flirt.

"Hey, Danielle," said Spencer.

"Hey, Spence."

"Where's your sister?"

"Home."

Danielle had a twin, Jessie. Both girls were excellent athletes—soccer and gymnastics, mostly. This spring they'd joined the track-and-field team and had become top sprinters and jumpers.

"Guess you came down here to see me," Spencer said with a sly smile. "Thanks for escorting her, Calvin. You can leave now."

"Nice try," Danielle said. "So what's going on today? You guys just lazing around like usual?"

"'Bout time we caught a break," Spencer replied. "Coach Wimmer has been driving us like a drill sergeant."

"I'm sure. Try training for the four-hundred-meters if you want to know tough."

"You saying track is harder than baseball?"

"Way harder," Danielle said. "What do you run, like, sixty feet between the bases or something? I'm barely getting started by that time."

"Yeah, well . . ." Spencer struggled to think of a response. "Baseball takes brains, too. Ain't that right, Ventura?"

Eddie nodded. He found it even harder to talk when there were cute girls around.

"Well," Danielle said, "I still think the real 'major talent' is on the track team."

Spencer changed the subject. "So, Calvin, what's it like to be such a powerful journalist?" he asked. "Making these judgments and assessments of all the teams?"

"I'm objective," Calvin said. "I just get some help from insiders."

Spencer turned to Eddie and smirked. "*Insiders,* he says. Maybe he just makes all that stuff up."

"Like what?" Calvin demanded.

"Like, I don't know. When you make fun of guys

on the team. I mean, I can take it, but it made poor little Ramiro here burst into tears when you questioned his singing ability."

Calvin gave an embarrassed laugh. "It's all documented."

"Can't wait to see the next one," Spencer said. "Probably be about Eddie hitting a foul ball or something."

"You'll have to wait and see," Calvin replied. He looked at Danielle and nodded his head toward the river. "See you chumps later," he said as they walked away.

"We'll be here. . . . Come on back, Danielle, if Calvin falls off a pier or something."

Eddie spread out on the grass then, the sun feeling great on his skin. "Didn't Calvin go out with Jessie once last summer?" he asked.

"Might have," Spencer said. "So did I. . . . Jessie's got a real edge, though. Danielle's always been sweeter."

Eddie leaned up on his elbows and looked over

at Calvin and Danielle walking on the path along the river. He couldn't imagine just hanging around with a girl, or especially going out for pizza or a movie. Guys like Spencer and Miguel were already shaving above their lips and had developed some muscles. They'd had girlfriends.

He just wasn't ready for any of that.

Life was complicated enough, with homework and chores and baseball. He knew things would change before too long, but for now he was glad to still be a kid.

8

A Pitcher's Nightmare

On Wednesday morning, Eddie grabbed a copy of the school paper as he entered his homeroom. He scanned the back page for the baseball article. He'd written it, of course, but it was always nice to actually see it in print.

WEDNESDAY, MAY 17

BASEBALL TEAM HOPES HOT STREAK LEADS TO POSTSEASON BERTH

By Major Talent

The Hudson City seventh-grade baseball team rolled to a pair of wins last week, inching closer to a spot in the league playoffs.

The regular season ends this week with games at Liberty this afternoon and at home against Weehawken on Friday. The Hornets beat both of those teams in earlier match-ups.

Hudson City has won seven of its past eight games, and its record stands at seven wins and five losses.

"We're a hot team right now, but we can't let our guard down," said Coach Wimmer after Friday's 5–2 win over Palisades.

Earlier in the week, the team had topped Memorial, 6–4. Both Palisades and Memorial had beaten the Hornets in early April.

"It's nice to get some payback on those teams—show them who's boss," said hot-hitting Spencer Lewis. Spencer, the shortstop and cleanup hitter, had a solo home run against Palisades and a two-run double in the win over Memorial.

Spencer made the defensive play of the year against Memorial, nabbing a line drive and turning a double play to kill a potential game-tying hit.

Catcher Jared Owen also homered against Palisades. The durable Owen has been behind the plate for every pitch this season.

"We don't even know who the second-string catcher is," said Spencer.

Apparently third baseman/pitcher Miguel Rivera would be the emergency catcher, according to Coach Wimmer. "I think he caught a few games in Little League," Coach said. "Let's just keep our fingers crossed that Jared doesn't get hurt. I don't think Miguel could pitch and catch in the same game. He'd have to be mighty quick!"

HORNET HAMMERINGS: First baseman Eddie "The Mouth" Ventura actually spoke recently. Coach Wimmer asked him how he was feeling, and Eddie said, "Fine." It was his longest conversation of the season. . . .

Center fielder Willie Shaw sat in gum after
striking out in the second inning against
Palisades. Ryan Grimes denied that the gum
was his, but he is the only one on the team
who likes grape-flavored chewing gum. . . .
Second baseman Lamont Wilkins was
caught listening to 1970s disco music on his
headset on the ride home from Memorial. . . .
Overlooked left-handed reliever Jimmy
Fleming plucked the splinters from his butt
and pitched key innings in both wins last
week.

"That wasn't disco!" Lamont said in the locker
room on Wednesday afternoon, pretending to be
angry. "It was my mom's CD. . . . I don't know how
it got in there."

"And that wasn't grape gum!" said Ryan. "It was
raspberry. . . . Not that it was mine anyway."

Eddie held back a smile. He could really throw
them off now. He stood up from the bench and
said, "And I gave a *two*-word reply to Coach! I

didn't say, 'Fine.' I said, '*I'm* fine.' Isn't that true, Coach?"

"Whatever you say, Eddie."

"See?"

A balled-up sock came flying across the room and just missed Eddie's head.

"There's one of my record-setting socks," Spencer said. "At least I got some good press for once, though. I'll have to tell Calvin to thank his 'source' for me." He looked right at Eddie when he said it, a knowing smile starting to form.

"Okay, hot shots," Coach said. "Get the uniforms on and start thinking about the baseball game. The bus to Jersey City leaves in five minutes."

Eddie was glad to see that Liberty had a different pitcher today. That short guy with the big curve was out in left field. Today's pitcher was tall and lean, with squinty eyes and a constant frown.

He was strong, too. Working quickly, with little hesitation, he struck out Lamont on three pitches to start the game. The entire at-bat lasted less than a minute.

Lamont was shaking his head as he walked past Eddie, who was kneeling in the on-deck circle.

"He's got good stuff," Lamont said.

Jared quickly fell behind, too. He managed to foul the third pitch back over the fence and out of play. But pitch number four caught him looking. He was out.

Big task for Ventura, but he's up for it. If anybody can figure out this pitcher, it's him.

"Hang in there," Jared said as he walked by. "There's a lot of zip on that ball."

The Liberty infield was making a lot of noise. They were up for a rout today; that loss to Hudson City two weeks before was not forgotten.

Eddie stepped to the plate and took an easy swing, his eyes never leaving the pitcher. He felt strangely calm; with two outs already and no one on base, there was less pressure to perform. And somehow that made him more confident that he would.

The first pitch had a lot of heat, but it was very high and inside. It was the first pitch this kid had thrown out of the strike zone all game. Eddie leaned back slightly as the ball whizzed by. It smacked off the top of the catcher's outstretched mitt and caromed into the backstop.

"Good eye," came the cry from the Hornets' dugout.

The catcher retrieved the ball and tossed it to the pitcher, calling, "Relax," as he threw it.

The pitcher's frown deepened into a sneer, but he nodded.

Eddie's batting average was not great—it had been hovering right around .200 all season—but he'd become better lately at anticipating pitches. This pitcher looked like a hothead; he probably had control issues. He'd follow that bad pitch with either another wild one or a much more conservative one. Eddie was ready for either.

You can't fool our boy Ventura. He's way too smart for that.

Here came the pitch he expected, fast but straight, right down the middle of the plate. It was the type Eddie feasted on in practice. He swung hard and felt the solid connection, and the ball darted out over the second baseman's head, falling safely into right field.

Eddie ran full speed to first base and held his ground.

The pitcher punched his fist into his glove and glared at Eddie.

Eddie smirked back. *Good,* he thought. *Go ahead and get mad. Throw another one into the backstop, why don't you?*

Spencer was at bat. Eddie took a big lead off first, ready to burst into a sprint. The next pitch was way outside and down in the dirt. Eddie was already running.

The catcher scooped up the ball and fired it toward second, but Eddie easily slid in with a stolen base. The Hornet players cheered loudly.

The catcher called time and walked to the mound, whispering to the pitcher.

This is almost too easy, Eddie thought. He was certain that the next pitch would be just like the one he had driven into the outfield.

Eddie was right. Spencer lined the ball up the middle and Eddie kept running. He rounded third and headed for home, easily scoring. He didn't even need to slide.

Miguel gave Eddie a one-armed hug, and Willie and Lamont met him at the dugout entrance with high fives and whoops.

"Smart base-running!" Coach Wimmer called. "Great job, Eddie."

Miguel hit a long fly ball to end the rally. But it was 1–0 Hudson City after half an inning. That had been the final score in the first meeting between the two teams.

Miguel put his bat back in the rack and grabbed his glove, walking to the mound. He'd been the winning pitcher in his previous two starts. Things were looking good for the Hornets.

Liberty scratched out a run in the bottom of the fourth on a walk, a bunt, and a single, tying the score at 1–1.

Coach Wimmer sent relief pitchers Velez and Fleming out to warm up as Hudson City came to bat in the fifth. Miguel was pitching well, but he appeared to be tiring.

Liberty still had its starting pitcher on the mound. He'd settled down after that first inning and had yielded only a couple of singles since.

The Hornets had the heart of their batting order coming up, with Jared leading off. Eddie settled into the on-deck circle and let out a deep breath.

Jared took a couple of pitches, then smacked a few foul balls. The next pitch was way inside, causing Jared to spin backwards to avoid getting hit. The next one was low. Jared had drawn a walk.

Lots of excitement in the ballpark as Eddie

Ventura steps to the plate. Ventura made this pitcher look like a Little Leaguer in the first inning. With a man on base, we're expecting more fireworks.

Eddie had grounded out on a sharply hit ball in the third inning, so he'd hit this guy's pitches well both times up. He felt more sure of himself than he ever had.

The pitcher scowled as he looked in for the catcher's sign. He glanced over at Jared, then reared back and fired a hard fastball.

The pitch looked outside to Eddie, but the umpire called a strike.

No problem, Eddie thought. *I've got this guy figured out.*

The next pitch was inside, but it was waist-high and looked fat. Eddie leaned back slightly and swung hard, driving the ball into right field again, this time closer to the foul line.

The right fielder raced to the ball and quickly threw to second base, ending any thoughts Eddie had of stretching the hit into a double. But Jared had advanced to third, in scoring position.

It was the first time all season Eddie'd had two hits in one game. His heart was racing.

The Liberty coach was walking to the mound.

That might be it for this guy. Ventura is a pitcher's nightmare. That hit had to shake the pitcher's confidence.

The coach jogged off the field without making a change. At home, Spencer took a massive practice swing, then tapped his bat on the plate.

Eddie took a short lead this time. He could hear Willie and David and the others shouting for Spencer to connect. A win over Liberty would just about wrap up a playoff spot for the Hornets.

The ball rocketed off Spencer's bat and flew high in the air toward center. The Liberty center fielder shaded his eyes with his hand as he edged toward the fence. Back to the wall, he made the catch. But Jared tagged up and scored.

The Hornets were ahead, 2–1.

After Miguel drew a walk, the Liberty coach visited the mound a second time, waving the left fielder in to pitch.

Eddie wasn't sure if this was good news or bad. They'd chased the starting pitcher and taken the lead, but this new pitcher had given them a hard time in the previous game.

Defense will make all the difference the rest of this game. Still only one out, though, so if Ventura can make it home from second, that third run would be huge.

But David struck out and Ryan hit a weak grounder to end the inning.

Eddie caught up to Miguel as they jogged toward the dugout to get their gloves. "Arm okay?" he asked.

"Sure. I still got some pitches in me."

"We gotta hold this lead."

"Tell me something I don't know."

Miguel walked the first batter, and a bunt moved him over to second. Up stepped the starting pitcher, scowling more than ever and eager to get some revenge.

Miguel threw a hard strike right past him, and the Hudson City infielders yelled. But then came a long series of balls and foul-offs, running the count to 3–2.

Eddie crouched lower and reminded himself to stay alert. Miguel took a big windup and threw with all his strength, but the pitch wasn't even close to the strike zone. The Liberty player rolled his bat toward the dugout and ran to first.

Two men on and only one out. Coach Wimmer called time and waved all of the infielders toward the mound.

"Great job, but I think you've had it," Coach said to Miguel.

Miguel gave a dark look as he handed Coach the ball.

"Smile, Miguel, things could be worse," Coach said. "Ryan, go out to right field. Miguel, take third."

Miguel did not smile, but his snarl went away.

Nobody ever stayed mad at Coach for more than a few seconds.

"Who's pitching?" Spencer asked.

Coach laughed gently. "Good question. Let's go with Velez." He turned to the dugout and pointed to Ramiro, motioning with a finger for him to take the field.

"Long way to go yet," Coach said to the infielders. "Everybody all right?"

The players nodded and said, "Yeah."

"Lot of pressure," Coach said. "Don't anybody puke on the field."

Coach could joke at the strangest times, but that made Eddie feel better. He relaxed. Being tense wouldn't help anyway.

Ramiro marched to the mound with a deadly serious expression. Coach gave him the ball and a light pat on the shoulder. "The fate of the world is on your shoulders," he said. "Try not to think about it too much."

The fielders yelled encouragement.

Down a run with men on first and second, it was unlikely that Liberty would be trying to steal bases. So Eddie stayed in his normal defensive spot, several feet from first base.

Ramiro got a quick strike on the batter, then nearly hit him with the next pitch. Jared made a great save, and the base runners held.

Eddie's eyes locked on the guy at first base. The kid looked amused for the first time all day. "This pitcher a little wild?" he asked Eddie.

Eddie looked away. "No more than you were."

Ramiro threw a second strike, then a third. It seemed as if the entire Hudson City team released a held breath at once. Two outs now. They might manage to keep the lead after all.

Batting now was that pitcher with the big curveball. He hadn't shown any power with the bat in the two games so far, but he'd had a couple of singles and hadn't struck out.

"Two outs!" called Spencer, holding up two fingers. "Force at any base."

Ramiro threw a fourth consecutive strike.

"Come on, Jamal," said the base runner, almost at a whisper. "Gotta bring us home."

Eddie glanced over at him. The kid smiled. "Heck of a game," he said, shaking his head in mock amazement.

Ramiro's next pitch was high and hard, and so was Jamal's swing. The ball flew on a line drive into deep right field, and it looked for a moment that it would be a home run.

The ball hit the top of the fence and bounced back onto the field. Ryan scrambled after it, but he'd chased it all the way to the fence and now had to backtrack.

The tying run was already in by the time Ryan threw the ball, and the other runner was on his way to the plate.

The throw was off line a bit, and Eddie had to lunge for it. But he caught it cleanly and pivoted in a hurry, throwing a strike toward Jared.

Jared grabbed the ball and turned, applying the

tag just as the sliding runner reached the plate.

The umpire thrust both arms out and called, "Safe!"

Jared stood and held the ball, his mouth hanging open. Ramiro shut his eyes and looked toward the sky. Eddie just stared at the celebrating Liberty players. They'd grabbed a one-run lead.

"Wake up!" Spencer called after a few seconds. "Let's get this third out and move on."

"Right back at 'em," said Lamont. "No batter."

Ramiro managed to get the next batter to pop out to Miguel at third. But the momentum had definitely shifted to Liberty's favor.

The Hornets did their best to gut things out and tie the game, but that Liberty pitcher was sharp. Hudson City went three up, three down in both the sixth and seven innings.

Eddie'd had his best game of the year, but it was hard to be happy after such a close loss. The team's fortunes had become more important to him than his own.

He knew that this team deserved a championship. But the season was a long way from over.

One thing seemed strange to him, though. That voice in his head had stopped talking when the game got really tight.

9

All or Nothing

The Hornets rebounded with a crucial win over Weehawken on Friday, securing a spot in the four-team playoffs. Eddie was totally focused on baseball now, and he'd had enough of pretending about who was writing the articles.

Besides, he'd had a great week. Two hits against Liberty and an RBI double against Weehawken. He deserved some attention for that.

EddieV: yo Calvin

HudCityCal: hey

EddieV: can you do the baseball article this
            week?

HudCityCal: how come?

EddieV: i think they're on 2 me

HudCityCal: who is?

EddieV: the team. my covers been blown

HudCityCal: no matter. its kind of obvious, no?

EddieV: what is?

HudCityCal: who MAJOR TALENT be

EddieV: but i made fun of myself last week. that
            should've fooled em.

HudCityCal: yeah. but those first 2 articles were all
            bout u

EddieV: so what do I do now?

HudCityCal: play it str8 4 one more article.

EddieV: you sure?

HudCityCal: yeah. I still need yur help. 1 more time.

EddieV: ok. but im keeping it short. cya later

"Another article for the paper?" Mrs. Ventura
said as she poked her head into the family room.

"Yeah. Kind of a wrap-up on last week and a pre-view of this one."

"The boys must be happy with the great pieces you've been writing."

Eddie swiveled in his chair to face his mom. "Well, they aren't supposed to know it's me. But some of them have figured it out, I think."

"I think you've done a wonderful job."

Eddie was surprised. "You read them?"

"Sure. They send copies over to our school so the teachers can see what their former students are up to. I had a lot of those kids in my class, remember? Spencer, Ramiro, Lamont."

"Yeah. How were they?"

Mom made a flapping motion with her fingers, indicating a mouth. "Boy, were they chatterboxes." She shook her head and smiled. "Nice kids, but Spencer especially—I sent him to the principal's office once a week at least."

"He doesn't shut up much now, either."

"He's got a good heart. Great energy. I never wanted

to thwart that, but some days he was too disruptive."

"He's a motor-mouth."

"Unlike someone we know." She put her hand on top of Eddie's head, then leaned over and kissed the back of his neck. "I'll leave you alone so you can work."

"Thanks, Mom. See you later."

Hudson City grabbed the fourth and final spot in the East Hudson League baseball playoffs with Friday's win over Weehawken. The Hornets will travel to Jersey City for a rematch with top-seeded Liberty in Thursday's opening round of the tournament.

Coach Wimmer sent David Choi out to pitch against Weehawken, and the righty responded with another outstanding performance. Plus, the Hornets' best hitters had big games, with Spencer Lewis and Miguel Rivera getting two extra-base hits apiece in the 6–1 victory.

Two days earlier, Liberty had edged Hudson City, 3–2, in a tense pitchers' duel. That loss had made the game with Weehawken a must-win situation for the Hornets.

"It was an all-or-nothing game for us," Coach Wimmer said after Friday's victory. "We win and we're in the play-offs; we lose and it's over. This is a tough league. There's not much margin for error."

Union City and Memorial also quali-fied for the league playoffs and will meet on Thursday. The two winners will decide the champion on Friday.

10

No Fear

"We beat them once, then they beat us," Spencer said, standing at the front of the bus before leading his teammates off. "I don't think there's any question about whose turn it is to win. Ours!"

"You heard him," Coach Wimmer added. "Assistant Coach Spencer says it's a done deal. I don't know why we're even bothering to play. They should probably just hand us the trophy."

"Just to prove it," Spencer said, "let's get out there."

The atmosphere was different than it had been last time the Hornets visited Jersey City just eight days before—totally charged with excitement. The Liberty bleachers were full this time, and a huge banner on the side of their dugout said LIBERTY IS WORTH FIGHTING FOR. The grass had been freshly mowed, and small flags were everywhere.

The two pitchers Hudson City had faced in earlier games were on the infield grass, tossing a ball back and forth. There were a few playful boos from the bleachers as the Hornets approached the field. They threw their sweatshirts and jackets onto the bench in the third-base dugout.

Eddie scanned the spectators and found his parents and Irene. He knew they would be there. But he was surprised to see his brother with them, too. Lenny stood up and lifted his fist as he caught Eddie's eye. Eddie gave the same gesture in return.

Coach pointed toward left field. "Out there," he said, and he started jogging that way, leading his players.

Spencer and Miguel put the team through some jumping jacks and other exercises, then made them drop for crunches. The players ran a few short sprints, then fell into pairs to throw baseballs back and forth.

Eddie noticed that his brother had moved down from the bleachers and was standing along the fence. He tossed the ball to Ramiro and jogged over.

Lenny reached out his hand and Eddie shook it.

"Had to cut a class, but I wouldn't miss this for anything," Lenny said. "Biggest game of your life, huh?"

"So far," Eddie said. "Tomorrow will be bigger... we hope."

"One at a time," Lenny said. "We're really proud of you."

"Me, too. Proud and nervous."

"Take a deep breath, little brother. In a lot of ways, it's just another game."

"Doesn't feel like it."

"Yeah, but make believe that it is. I mean, play harder than you ever played in your life, but keep your wits about you. You hear me?"

"Yeah." Eddie nodded and looked back at the field. David was throwing hard now, zeroing in to get ready to pitch. Lamont and Spencer looked intense as can be as they stretched near third base. Miguel was sitting on the ground, reaching for his toes, staring at the backstop.

Lenny had been through this sort of playoff pressure a million times. It was easy for him to say things like that. But Eddie knew he was right. The clutch players always came through, no matter how much pressure they were under.

Jamal—the shorter guy with the big curve—was pitching for Liberty, but he'd learned not to be so rigid with his pattern. And he'd added a decent change-up to the curve and his fastball. The Hornets went three straight innings without getting a base runner.

David had been efficient as well, but Liberty had squeaked across a pair of runs by capitalizing on two walks, a throwing error by Spencer, and a bloop single into right. So the Hornets were down, 2–0, as they came to bat in the fourth, even though Liberty had managed only one base hit.

Eddie leaned against the dugout fence as Lamont strode to the plate. Lamont had been in a bit of a slump, and he'd struck out to start the game.

He took Jamal's first pitch for a strike, but smashed the second one deep into left-center. Eddie stood on tiptoes to see over his teammates, and he felt a surge of energy as the ball cleared the fence for a home run.

Lamont leaped high into the air as he rounded first base, breaking into a huge smile. Several Hornets left the dugout to slap hands with Lamont as he rounded third. Eddie and Jared met him at the plate with big embraces.

The pitcher stood with his hands on his hips, a blank stare on his face. The umpire tossed him a new baseball, and he caught it in his bare hand.

"Jared!" yelled Spencer. "Keep this thing going, buddy!"

Suddenly it seemed like a different pitcher out there. He threw four bad pitches to Jared, putting the tying run on first base.

Eddie took a deep breath and bent down to wipe some dirt off his shoe. Then he stared at the pitcher until he made eye contact. Eddie allowed himself to smile slightly, letting this guy know he had no fear at all.

The Liberty coach called time out and walked to the mound. He spoke calmly to his pitcher and tapped him on the shoulder. Then he jogged off the field, adjusting his glasses as he went.

Eddie looked over at Jared and nodded. Things just felt right all of a sudden.

The pitch was fast and a little low, just over the outside of the plate. Eddie made a nice smooth swing and felt the bat crush the ball, sending it zinging in the air toward the gap between the right and center fielders.

Jared had been running on the pitch and was nearly to third by the time Eddie turned for second. The shortstop was on second base waiting for the throw. Eddie dove with his hands outstretched, reaching for the bag. He tasted dirt, but he grabbed the base just before he felt the tag. He was safe, and Jared had scored to tie the game!

Eddie stood up and looked toward the dugout, where his teammates were yelling his name and pointing. He blushed and bit down on his lip. The front of his jersey was a nice reddish brown.

He looked toward the bleachers this time and saw his parents and Irene and Lenny, standing and cheering. He'd never had a moment like this one.

The Liberty coach was back on the mound now. That pitcher was history. The big guy with the scowl was on his way in from left field.

It seemed premature to Eddie that they'd be changing pitchers already. After all, the starter had been unhittable until this inning. But then again, this was the playoffs. Whichever team lost was finished.

Spencer grounded the first pitch to first, advancing Eddie to third. Now he could see his friends in the dugout close up. Lamont—so charged up from that home run—was banging on the fence with his mitt and yelling for Miguel to bring Eddie home. Willie had his hands cupped around his mouth and was shouting for a hit. Jared and Ryan were both hollering, too.

And when Miguel hit a deep fly ball to right, Eddie tagged up and waited. As soon as the catch was made, he put his head down and sprinted toward home plate, sliding for the second time in the inning and scoring the go-ahead run.

The entire team mobbed Eddie as he jogged back to the dugout.

"We got the lead, man!" shouted Spencer. "We got the lead."

"Somebody get Eddie a new uniform!" Willie joked. "He's brown from head to toe."

Eddie picked up his mitt and tried to catch his breath. David struck out to end the inning, but the

Hornets suddenly looked like a very tough team to beat.

David continued pitching well, but Liberty made the most of its few opportunities. After yielding an infield single in the fifth, David struck out two batters and then issued a walk on a very close 3–2 pitch.

Liberty stunned everyone by attempting a double steal on the next pitch. Jared hesitated as he stood with the ball, not sure whether to throw to second or third. That split second cost him, as the throw to Miguel at third base was late by a couple of inches.

Coming through in the clutch, Jamal made up for his earlier pitching lapse and stroked a neat single into center. Both runners scored, and Liberty had regained the lead, 4–3.

David seemed to lose his nerve after that. He walked the next batter. And it took a great play by Spencer on a grounder up the middle to finally end the inning.

Coach gave David a firm pat on the back as the team came off the field. But Ramiro and Jimmy were already warming up. David threw his mitt onto the bench and sat down.

Eddie walked to lead off the sixth and reached third when Miguel doubled. But the brief rally went nowhere as David struck out again and Rico Cabrera hit a weak grounder to first.

Jimmy Fleming came on to pitch a perfect inning in the bottom of the sixth, keeping Hudson City just one run behind.

"Last ups," Spencer said as they reached the dugout. "Let's make it count."

The bottom of the order was coming to bat for Hudson City—Ryan and then Willie. The Hornets would need two base runners or Eddie wouldn't bat. It might not happen.

Ryan grounded out, but Willie knocked a single up the middle, and the Hornets' spectators came to life again.

Lamont stepped up to the plate with plenty of confidence. He'd homered earlier and nearly had another, sending the Liberty center fielder all the way to the fence.

Lamont took a couple of fierce practice swings. One more good connection and the Hornets could be back in the lead.

He got ahead of the first pitch and sent it deep toward left, but it drifted foul and brought about a groan from the Hornets' dugout.

He fouled off the second pitch, too, sending it straight up and over the backstop.

Eddie put on a batting helmet and held his breath. Lamont took a powerful cut at the next pitch, but to no avail. He shut his eyes and jutted his head forward, then walked back to the dugout. Two outs.

But Jared drew a walk. The tying and leading runs were on base.

And Eddie was coming to bat.

He'd been hitting well lately, but the pressure in

this situation was ten times higher than he'd felt before. Every eye really was on him now. The fate of his team was all up to him.

His hands were sweating, but suddenly his forehead felt clammy and cold. His throat was tight and dry. His teammates were screaming from the dugout. The Liberty fielders were yelling.

The scowling pitcher was almost smiling now, looking confident and ready.

Eddie inhaled deeply and glanced up at Jared and Willie on the bases, tensed and ready to run. He looked toward the dugout and saw Lenny leaning on the fence nearby. And the sight of his brother made him instantly feel calmer—the Venturas had been in situations like this before. They'd always come through.

The first pitch was low and outside, and Eddie let it go by for a ball. He moved his shoulders back and forth to get looser, then pulled back the bat and gripped it tighter.

The second pitch was low and inside, but the

umpire called it a strike. That pumped up the Liberty side even more. Cries of "Easy out!" and "No batter!" erupted.

This is the pitch, Eddie told himself. *This is the season, right here.*

And he was ready. The ball had some spin on it, curving into the strike zone at a perfect height and trajectory for Eddie's swing. He walloped the pitch, and it took off on a hard line drive.

Straight at the second baseman.

The Liberty players charged toward the mound as the ball was caught, leaping and shouting in celebration of the win. Eddie stopped short halfway up the first-base path, stunned and frozen. He stared at the player who'd caught the ball.

Jared walked by on his way to the dugout, blinking back tears. Willie was kneeling between second and third base, shaking his head.

Eddie felt a hand on his shoulder. "Game over," said Spencer. "Game over."

ll

Special Edition

The bus was quiet on the way back to Hudson City. The players couldn't believe that their season was done.

Coach offered some words of encouragement before they got off the bus, but most of the players were shocked by the sudden ending to what had been a great run.

Miguel stood up.

"Team party Friday night in the back room at El Torito," he said. "We had hoped it would be a championship celebration, but we can still be proud. You can invite one guest apiece." A small smile brightened his face. "Hopefully a few of us will invite girls. If you don't have any friends, tough luck. Just get there yourself."

Miguel swallowed hard, choking back a tear. "My aunt and uncle are providing food and soda, and my parents are buying pizzas from Villa Roma. Anybody who doesn't like Mexican food or pizza can bring a peanut-butter sandwich, I guess. And if your parents want to send some cookies or brownies, that'd be great, too."

Spencer started to clap, and a few others joined in. "Great season," Spencer said. "I mean it."

"Great *team*," added David. "I wouldn't trade you guys for anything."

Eddie nodded, but he couldn't speak. The feeling of that final line drive was embedded in him now. He kept reliving it—the surge of energy and joy as the bat met the ball, feeling so solid and certain to bring one run home if not two. The lightning-quick end to all of those good emotions as the ball went straight into the fielder's mitt.

The disappointment on his teammates' faces.

The knowledge that the difference between a win and a loss had been tiny.

When Eddie entered the cafeteria the following day for lunch, he was surprised to find small stacks of papers on each table. It was a one-page edition of the school newspaper.

Jared and Willie were eating their lunch and reading the paper. Eddie sat down to join them.

HORNET HIGHLIGHTS
SPECIAL EDITION

FRIDAY, MAY 26

LIBERTY OUSTS HC FROM PLAYOFFS
INSPIRING SEASON ENDS WITH ONE-RUN LOSS

By Calvin Tait, Sports Editor

JERSEY CITY—A terrific season-ending run came to a heartbreaking end for the

Hudson City seventh-grade baseball team Thursday. Top-seeded Liberty Junior High School edged the Hornets, 4–3, in the first round of the East Hudson League playoffs.

Hudson City had overcome the adversity of a four-game losing streak to start the season, winning eight of its final ten games before Thursday's loss. The Hornets deserve a lot of credit for keeping their heads up during the dark days of early April and rebounding with a great stretch of baseball.

"Liberty's good," team leader Spencer Lewis stated in an e-mail message Thursday night. "They beat us twice in the past week, so I guess they deserve to be playing for the title. It's painful for us, but what can you do?"

Liberty will host second-seeded Union City in the championship game this afternoon.

David Choi pitched a solid game for the

Hornets Thursday, taking the loss despite yielding just three hits in five innings.

"Liberty is a hard team to get out," Choi said Thursday evening, also via e-mail. "They're patient, so they draw a lot of walks, and they make the most of every base runner. I think we showed that we're a great team, too. It could have gone either way."

Lamont Wilkins had a towering home run for the Hornets to spark a fourth-inning rally. Jared Owen and Eddie Ventura also scored as the Hornets briefly took the lead.

HORNET HAMMERINGS: Jimmy Fleming pitched one shutout inning in relief Thursday. . . . Choi struck out six hitters, but he also struck out twice himself. . . . Special thanks to quiet first baseman Ventura, who provided invaluable insights for our baseball coverage this season!

"Not a bad article," said Miguel, who was reading over Eddie's shoulder. "He didn't mention my double, but it's a pretty good wrap-up on the season."

"He revealed me as the source!" Eddie said.

"You weren't fooling anybody anymore," said Willie.

"Guess not."

"I guess I ought to invite Calvin to the team party," Miguel said. He turned to Eddie and squinted a little, nodding. "I mean, the coverage of the team *was* pretty good this season."

Eddie shrugged. He'd take that as a compliment. Why continue to hide behind an illusion? He could play baseball and he could write articles. And anyone who wanted to judge either performance was welcome to do so. He was proud of what he'd done—on the field and in print.

As he walked down the hallway toward his next class, Eddie became aware of a familiar voice in his head. He hadn't heard it for a while, and he'd missed it. That voice was a big part of who he was.

All in all, it's been a pretty good year for this kid Ventura, the voice was saying. *We're expecting big things in coming seasons. Be sure to stay tuned for more.*

* * *

RICH WALLACE

was a high school and college athlete and then a sportswriter before he began writing novels. He is the author of many critically acclaimed sports-themed novels, including *Wrestling Sturbridge*, *Shots on Goal*, and *Restless: A Ghost's Story*. Wallace lives with his family in Honesdale, Pennsylvania.